GW00863455

Littlenose and Two-Eyes

Littlenose and Two-Eyes

John Grant

Illustrated by the author

AS TOLD IN JACKANORY

BRITISH BROADCASTING CORPORATION

Published by the
British Broadcasting Corporation
35 Marylebone High Street
London WIM 4AA

First published 1985

ISBN 0 563 20364 1
© John Grant 1985

Typeset by Phoenix Photosetting, Chatham

Printed and bound in England
by Mackays of Chatham Ltd

Contents

Littlenose
and Two-Eyes

Littlenose sat under his favourite tree. Two-Eyes
was sitting beside him, and for once Littlenose
paid no attention to the little mammoth. Even
when Two-Eyes gave a squeak and prodded
Littlenose with his trunk, Littlenose brushed it
aside and said, "Don't bother me, Two-Eyes. I'm
busy, can't you see?"

Two-Eyes *couldn't* see, and he got to his feet and
went off in a huff.

Littlenose settled back against the tree, closed
his eyes, and began mumbling to himself. He was
learning a poem. It had all started a week ago. To
everyone's surprise, not least of all Littlenose's,
he had passed each of his tests for promotion

from apprentice to junior hunter. Actually he had one more test to do, which was the reason for the poem. He had passed fire-lighting with distinction, tracking with top marks, and spear throwing . . . just! But now he had the last and final test. It was called Hunting the Grey Bear.

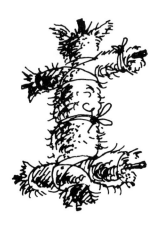

There wasn't really a grey bear, or any other colour of bear for that matter. Three pieces of wood were tied together in a special way and covered with grey fur. This was carefully hidden, and the apprentice hunter had to find it by following clues.

The clues formed a poem, and it was this that Littlenose was memorising. It didn't seem to make a lot of sense, which didn't make it any easier to learn:

The Grey Bear's prints are in the clay,
The noon-day shadow points the way,
The island's where the heron cries,
The ashwood close on willow lies,
The peak where pine grows to the sky,
The Grey Bear in his den does lie!

Littlenose said it once through to himself, then once more out loud. As long as he remembered it tomorrow, all he had to do was work out what it all meant.

Next morning Littlenose was up before it was
light. After a quick breakfast he hurried to the
Old Man's cave carrying his boy-size spear. There
was quite a crowd of hunters waiting to see him
off. Father wasn't there. He had gone off even
earlier with another man to hide the Grey Bear.
The Old Man made a short speech about how he
hoped that Littlenose's name would be inscribed
on the birch-bark roll of junior hunters. Then he
gave Littlenose a tightly-wrapped package, food
for the day "not to be eaten until the third line of
the poem".

Littlenose took the package, said thank you,
and set off while everyone shouted: "GOOD
LUCK!"

As he left the caves behind he was quite sure of the first clue. The only clay around was close to the river and was used by the Neanderthal folk for making pots and bowls. Sure enough, there was a line of marks in the clay that looked more or less like bear prints. As he looked there was a noise, and out from among the trees trotted Two-Eyes.

"Go home," shouted Littlenose. "You can't come. This is all very important."

The little mammoth looked very crestfallen, and Littlenose turned his back and began to hurry along the line of tracks. The tracks left the clay, but Littlenose found them easily as they crossed grassy patches, led through the pinewoods, and took him far across a sandy heath.

Then they stopped. Just like that!

What was the next line of the poem?

The noon-day shadow points the way.

What shadow? Which way? It was almost noon now. He stood, perplexed. Then there was a quiet snuffle behind him. He jumped round.

"Two-Eyes!" he shouted. "What do you mean, following me like that? This is work for hunters, not mammoths!"

He started to think again about noon-day shadows, when Two-Eyes squeaked once more. He was standing pointing with his trunk to something on the ground. Right where the bear tracks ended was a rock. "That's no good," said Littlenose. "It's too sunken in the grass to cast a shadow." Two-Eyes pointed again with his trunk. The rock was chipped and cracked, and in the centre was a hole slightly bigger than a finger. "Of course," cried Littlenose. "You are a clever mammoth!"

He took his spear and stuck it upright in the hole in the rock. It was noon. The shadow of the spear lay along the grass, and at its tip was a white stone. A few steps away was another, then another. If he went from stone to stone he should come to: *The island's where the heron cries*. He hoped it wasn't too far. He couldn't open his packed lunch till then, and he was getting hungry.

The white stones led in a wandering way over open country. Ahead, Littlenose could see low trees and bushes and the glint of water. As he got nearer, the ground underfoot grew damp. There were stagnant pools and clumps of reeds. He came to the end of the trail of white stones and found himself on the edge of a wide marsh. A broad, slow-flowing river lay across his path.

Littlenose and Two-Eyes splashed the short distance to the river. There were willow trees along the bank, and others growing on a couple of islands. Which was the island with the herons, he wondered?

Two-Eyes nudged him with his trunk.
Littlenose turned. A heron was pacing
majestically through the shallows by the bank. It
stood still for several moments, peering down into
the water. Then, quick as a flash, its long beak
darted into the water and came up with a
wriggling fish. Littlenose watched. The heron
slipped the fish into its crop, then rose into the
air on enormous wings. It circled round and
dropped down into the top of a tree on the
farthest-away island. "That's it," said Littlenose.
"That's the one!"

Followed by a reluctant mammoth – Two-Eyes didn't like getting his fur wet – Littlenose waded into the river. The water was little more than knee deep, and they quickly reached the island. There were several heron nests in the trees, and the big birds screeched at the intruders.

"Well, the herons are crying, all right," said Littlenose. "That's the third line of the poem. Now I can eat my lunch." He opened the tightly-wrapped skin package. The Old Man had given him several pieces of prime venison. But . . . it was raw! It must be part of the test. All he had to do was build a fire.

It came as a nasty shock to find that there seemed to be nothing to build a fire *with*! The island was low-lying and swampy, and the few twigs and sticks Littlenose found lying in the grass were too wet to burn. Again, it was Two-Eyes who came to the rescue. He went over to one of the trees and reached up with his trunk. The branches were loaded with dead grass and sticks brought down in the winter floods, all perfectly dry. Littlenose stood on Two-Eyes' back and dragged down an armful. Quickly he struck a light with his flints, and in a short time the venison was toasting over the flames.

Fed and contented, Littlenose sat on a low willow branch and thought, while Two-Eyes grazed nearby. That was half the clues used up, although he had to admit that without Two-Eyes' help he wouldn't have done so well! Why, if he weren't a mammoth he might make a pretty good hunter himself. What was the next part of the poem?

The ashwood close on willow lies.

That wasn't much help. There was plenty of willow. In fact there was nothing else. Where did the bit about "ash" fit in? Was it perhaps among the driftwood in the trees? Oh, dear! What if he'd burnt it in his cooking fire! He jumped down and picked up his spear. And as he did so he remembered, the Neanderthal Folk used ash for spear and axe handles. It must mean his spear. Another thought struck him, and he climbed back on to the willow branch. Yes! He'd wondered about the fresh marks cut in the bark. They were made just where small branches formed forks. He took the spear and rested it in the forks. It fitted perfectly, as if they were made for it . . . which they probably were! And the spear pointed straight back across the river towards a distant hill. That's where he had to go now.

The hill was farther away than Littlenose first thought and it was late afternoon before he came near its foot. It was really a small mountain. The

lower slopes were quite bare – they seemed to consist of red gravel. Higher up was red rock. The rock formed weird peaks and pinnacles.

The peak where pine grows to the sky,
The Grey Bear in his den does lie!

And there, just visible against the sky, was the twisted shape of an ancient pine clinging to the summit of one of the pinnacles. There was the end of the trail. Somewhere up there were three pieces of wood tied together in a strange fashion and covered with grey fur. All he had to do was climb up and get it.

Littlenose strained his eyes to find an easy route to the summit. He paused. He could see people. Two figures seemed to be hiding behind one of the smaller pinnacles lower down. Of course! That would be Father and his friend who had hidden the Grey Bear. He would pretend he hadn't seen them.

Littlenose and Two-Eyes circled round the base of the hill. And to their delight they found that a path led almost to the top. Up they went, arriving panting close under the pine tree. It grew out of a crack above Littlenose's head, but the rock seemed quite unclimbable. They stood precariously at the top of the gravel slope and wondered where on earth the Grey Bear could be hidden.

While Littlenose poked about, Two-Eyes had been looking down to the foot. He gave a sudden soft squeak. "What is it?" said Littlenose. "Have you found it?"

He followed Two-Eyes' gaze . . . and his heart
almost stopped. Half-way up, a huge black bear
stood, rearing up on its hind legs. It had been
hidden from below by the rocks. That was why
Father and his friend were hiding! Not from
Littlenose. The bear took a couple of steps, but
the gravel slipped under its feet. It couldn't get at
the hunters, but it was prepared to wait!

"We must do something, Two-Eyes," said
Littlenose. And he pulled himself up on to part of
the rock for a better view. Too late he realised
that the rock was loose. He flung himself to one
side as the rock crashed down the hill. He fell
against Two-Eyes and together they rolled down
after the rock in a great cloud of red dust.

The bear leapt back in fright. What was this? A landslide . . . and a cloud of dust that made a noise like an angry mammoth! To crown it all a large rock bounced out from the dust cloud just missing the bear's head. Without a backward glance it turned and fled.

As the dust cleared, Father and the other man ran to join Littlenose and Two-Eyes. "That was one of the bravest things I've ever seen," said Father. "And, of course, congratulations!" Littlenose looked down. Brought down with the stones and gravel and lying at his feet was the Grey Bear.

That night Littlenose stood proudly as the Old Man took a piece of charcoal and made the marks on the roll of junior hunters that meant "Littlenose". Father whispered something in the Old Man's ear. The Old Man smiled and added: "and Two-Eyes".

"You two really are a team," he said.

"I knew Two-Eyes would make a hunter," thought Littlenose. Then he hurried home, hoping that being a junior hunter meant that he was now allowed to stay up late with the grown-ups.

The Amber Pendant

Next to the Old Man, who was Chief, the most important person in Littlenose's tribe was the Doctor. And this was not only because he cured people when they were sick, but because he was also a magician! Everyone was a bit afraid of the Doctor. Some said that he wasn't Neanderthal at all. That was why he never appeared without the ceremonial mask which hid his face. Some even went as far as to say that he was really a Straightnose – which explained why he was so clever.

The Doctor had a wife. And she was even more of a mystery. By Neanderthal standards she was almost unbelievably ugly. Her hair was long and golden, which gave her her name: Goldie. And her nose was not much bigger than Littlenose's. She rarely ventured from her cave, and the people said that the Doctor was ashamed of her. Of course, they didn't say that to his face. You don't go around talking about someone whose husband could easily turn you into a frog . . . or worse.

One evening Father came home and said, "The Doctor's wife has lost an amber pendant. He's offering a reward to whoever finds it."

Littlenose looked up from his supper. "I bet I find it," he said. "What's a pendant?"

"She wears it around her neck," said Father. "Two pieces of amber on a leather thong."

"I see," said Littlenose. "And what's amber?"

Father sighed. He thought for a moment. "It's yellow stuff. With flies in it. And it's magic."

Littlenose tried to picture it for himself. Yellow? Flies? All he could think about was egg yolk – with greedy flies getting their legs stuck. And magic? Magic egg yolk? He tried to imagine the Doctor's wife wearing two runny eggs covered with flies. Grown-ups were even odder people than he thought! But the reward! He didn't care *what* he found as long as he got the reward.

First thing after breakfast next day he set off
with Two-Eyes to hunt for the missing amber
pendant. And it was a lot more difficult than he
had imagined. Littlenose thought that all he had
to do was keep his eyes open for something
yellow. He said so to Two-Eyes. "Then we check
it for the flies," he said.

Two-Eyes sighed. Life with Littlenose was
never dull, but it was sometimes hard for a young
mammoth to understand what was going on.

They walked along by the river. People often
lost things while they were fishing or just out
walking, thought Littlenose. He peered at the
ground and at the shallow water near the bank.
Then he stopped. "Look, Two-Eyes!" he cried.
Something bright and yellow shone among the
small waves. He jumped down the bank. And saw
that it was only the sunlight shining on the
pebbles. Ah, well! Better luck next time!

Then it was Two-Eyes' turn. He gave a squeak and pointed with his trunk. In the shadow of a tree were two, bright yellow objects. Littlenose rushed to pick them up. But before he had got half-way the two objects rose into the air and fluttered away among the trees. "Butterflies!" cried Littlenose. "You really are stupid, Two-Eyes!"

"He's a fine one to talk," muttered Two-Eyes in mammoth language, as they went on their way.

They came out of the trees into a wide clearing on the far side of which was a high outcrop of rock. And in the face of the rock was what looked like the opening of a cave. It looked promising as a place to find lost property. In any case, Littlenose liked exploring, despite the number of times he had been warned about going into strange caves.

Littlenose walked boldly into the dark entrance, but Two-Eyes hung back. His mammoth senses told him that all was not well. Reluctantly, with a bit of persuasion, he followed Littlenose. And Littlenose had only taken a few steps when he stopped. At the back of the cave were two brightly-shining yellow objects. Littlenose could hardly believe his luck! It couldn't be the sun shining this time. And butterflies didn't live in caves. Then he paused. One of the yellow objects had disappeared for a moment. Almost as if it had blinked. "I must have imagined it," thought Littlenose. "This is certainly my lucky day!"

"This is certainly *my* lucky day," thought the sabre-tooth tiger. It had been having a quiet nap at the back of the cave when Littlenose had come charging in. Here, before its very eyes was its favourite mid-morning snack: fresh, tender Neanderthal boy, walking straight up to it! So as not to waste a moment, the sabre-tooth tiger opened its jaws wide, and waited.

Littlenose jumped as underneath the two bright shining objects appeared two rows of bright shining white teeth. And as he grew accustomed to the dim light in the cave he made out the shape of a sabre-tooth tiger! He was too terrified to move, even when the tiger rose to its feet and began to purr at the thought of fresh boy. Then it jumped back, startled. It hadn't seen Two-Eyes' dark fur among the shadows. But now the little mammoth trumpeted as loud as he could. The echoes in the cave made it sound like a whole herd. And when the tiger saw a red eye and a green eye shining out at it it didn't know what to think. Before it could make up its mind Littlenose and Two-Eyes were out of the cave and running like the wind. They didn't stop until they were close to the caves where the tribe lived.

They knew the tiger would not pursue them
there, so they sat down under a willow tree to
recover their breath. Littlenose put his hand on
the ground and felt something in the grass. It was
a rabbit's paw . . . but without the rabbit.
Someone had taken the trouble to bind it round
with strips of leather, and there was a loop as if it
were meant to hang on something. "Strange,"
thought Littlenose. "Perhaps Uncle Redhead will
know what it's for." And he tucked it into the
secret pocket in his furs.

But he was no nearer finding the amber
pendant. "Come on, Two-Eyes," he said. "It will
soon be lunchtime. Let's have one more look."

Littlenose started off, but it was marshy ground
and Two-Eyes didn't like to get his fur wet. He
went the long way round. Suddenly, Littlenose
heard him squeal. The little mammoth was
standing pointing with his trunk. Littlenose ran to
join him. He couldn't see anything at first, but the
breeze stirred a clump of rushes and he caught a
quick glimpse of something bright yellow. Again
he splashed through the pools of water . . . and
found himself looking at a clump of marsh
marigolds. The bright yellow blooms nodded in
the wind and made reflections in the water.

That was it, decided Littlenose. Reward or no reward, he had had enough of lost amber pendants. It was almost lunchtime. If he could think of nothing better to do he would start looking again in the afternoon . . . perhaps! Mother liked flowers, though, and it would be nice to take a bunch back to her. Littlenose picked a big bouquet of marsh marigolds and set off home.

He was almost there when he realised that he
was close to the cave where the Doctor lived with
his ugly wife. There was the cave, and someone
was moving about outside. It was Goldie. She was
preparing her husband's lunch, and sat on a rock
in the sunshine plucking a pigeon. Littlenose
knew that it was rude to stare, but he went closer
and stopped to look at Goldie. She wasn't really
all *that* ugly, even if she did have golden hair
instead of the dark Neanderthal variety. And
small noses weren't a total disaster, thought
Littlenose, touching his own.

Suddenly Goldie looked up. She smiled.
"You're Littlenose, aren't you?" she said.

"Yes," said Littlenose, "and . . ."

"And you've brought me flowers!" cried Goldie.

"Well, really . . ." began Littlenose. Then he
stopped and handed the bunch of marsh
marigolds to her. "I've been out all morning
looking for your amber pendant," he said. "And I
haven't found it."

"I'm not surprised," replied Goldie. "It was never lost. The Doctor had no sooner offered the reward than I found it lying where it had fallen in a dark corner of the cave. I don't suppose he's got round to telling people yet. I'm sorry you were put to so much trouble. Would you like to see it?"

Littlenose nodded, not quite sure. Goldie went into the cave and came out carrying what looked like two large golden pebbles strung on a leather thong. But they weren't pebbles. Littlenose could see right inside them.

"Take them," said Goldie. "Look at the insects trapped inside." Littlenose drew back. "Don't be afraid," said Goldie.

"What about the magic?" asked Littlenose fearfully.

"Oh, that," laughed Goldie. "I'll show you in a moment."

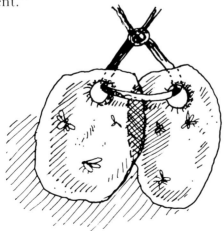

Littlenose took the pendant in his hand and
held it up. True enough, there were several small
flies and midges embedded in the amber. Goldie
took the pendant again and rubbed one of the
pieces of amber vigorously against her furs. Then
she held it over some of the small feathers
plucked from the pigeon. And as Littlenose
watched, the feathers floated upwards and clung
to the amber.

"That's it," said Goldie. "Not very useful magic." Littlenose nodded agreement. "Well, I must get on," said Goldie. "A cavewife's work is never done. Thank you for calling. And for the flowers. Goodbye."

He was at his own cave when he remembered
the rabbit's paw he had found. He must
remember to ask Uncle Redhead about it next
time he visited. He took it out of his pocket and
was walking head down examining it when he
bumped into someone. It was Nosey, the Chief
Tracker of the tribe.

"Can't you watch where you're going?" he
shouted. "You youngsters have no consideration!
In my young day . . . hi! What's that you've
got there?"

"I found it," said Littlenose.

"Clever lad! Clever lad!" shouted Nosey. "My lucky rabbit's foot! I've been lost without it! How can I ever repay you? Here!" And he thrust a handful of coloured pebbles at Littlenose, enough to buy all sorts of good things at the next market.

Littlenose stood deep in thought. What a strange day it had been! He had almost been eaten by a sabre-tooth tiger looking for a pendant that wasn't lost. And now he had a reward for finding a piece of dead rabbit.

"Come on, Two-Eyes," he said. "Let's see what's for lunch."

Littlenose the Swinger

It was an evening in early autumn. Uncle
Redhead was visiting for a few days, and he sat
with Father, Mother and Littlenose as they were
finishing their evening meal. Uncle Redhead
patted his stomach. "Congratulations on an
excellent repast," he said.

Mother blushed, and said, "Oh, it was nothing.
Just scraps, you know."

"You call that scraps?" said Uncle Redhead.
"Grilled woolly rhinoceros with watercress?
Smoked salmon steaks? Bramble and crab-apple
salad? Scraps?" He looked at Father. Father only
grunted something. He thought that Uncle
Redhead talked too much . . . among other things.
Littlenose just sat back feeling full.

Mother spoke again. "I could make something *really* special if I had some pheasant. I was given this recipe by Mrs Nosey."

"No problem," said Uncle Redhead. "Pheasant season's just started. We'll go tomorrow. First thing. Couple of brace be enough?"

Littlenose lay awake for a long time that night. He could hardly remember eating pheasant. And he knew why. Pheasants were very hard to catch. They flew fast, either too far overhead for a spear to reach them, or so close to the ground that it was difficult to spot them against the undergrowth and long grass. Littlenose wondered if his uncle had some special pheasant-hunting method. He would find out in the morning.

But he didn't. He awoke to the sound of rain drumming down outside the cave. The hunt was off. There was nothing much to do but sit around the fire and tell stories to pass the time. And Mother put a stop to that. Some of Uncle Redhead's stories, she said, were quite unsuitable for the ears of a child.

So Uncle Redhead amused them with tricks and games he had picked up on his travels. He had three seashells which he laid on a flat rock. There was a berry under one of the shells, and no matter how hard they tried no one could guess which one it was. Father got angry and called it childish nonsense.

So Uncle Redhead made shadows with his
hands in the firelight against the wall of the cave.
He made birds and mammoths and horses. And a
very lifelike sabre-tooth tiger. Littlenose shouted
with delight, but Father turned his back
muttering about overgrown children.

That night Father said to Mother, "I don't
think Redhead's a good influence on Littlenose.
It's no way for a grown man to behave."

The following morning dawned bright and
clear. After breakfast Father and Uncle Redhead
got ready for the hunt. "We'll take Littlenose
along," said Uncle Redhead. "It will be good
experience for him."

"Huh! Two children instead of one!" muttered
Father.

The pheasant wood was some considerable distance from the cave, and it was late afternoon before they reached it. Littlenose was sent into the wood while the two men waited in the open ground. At Uncle Redhead's command Littlenose began his part in the operation. He walked forward shouting and clapping his hands. Nothing happened for a moment. Then, with a clatter of wings, a large cock pheasant burst out of the bushes in front of him. It was followed by another. And another. Within a few moments half a dozen of the big, brightly-coloured birds had taken to the air. They shot out from the cover of the wood towards a waiting Father and Uncle Redhead. Alas, as usual, they were too fast! Father's spear came close, and knocked out a few tail feathers from one bird, but after giving an angry squawk it flew away otherwise unharmed.

Littlenose came out of the wood. "Where's all the pheasants, then?" he asked.

After a rest they tried again in another part of the wood. They tried another three times altogether. And they hadn't a single pheasant to show for it.

The sun was beginning to set so they decided to camp for the night. Their luck might be better tomorrow. Father and Uncle Redhead rested by the fire, but Littlenose thought he would have a last play. He strolled among the trees, wondering how to amuse himself.

Some way into the wood, Littlenose saw a special tree which gave him a wonderful idea. A long, springy branch grew outwards from the trunk, and Littlenose climbed up and hung by his hands. Then he began to bounce up and down, and in a few moments he was laughing with excitement as the branch whipped to and fro and Littlenose went up and down with it.

Back at the camp-fire Uncle Redhead thought that he would like a little walk. Father couldn't be bothered, so Uncle Redhead went alone. He heard Littlenose long before he saw him. "What are you doing?" he asked, when he saw Littlenose dangling on the end of the branch.

"It's a swing," said Littlenose. "I'm swinging!"

"Call that swinging?" said Uncle Redhead scornfully. "That's just bouncing on an old tree branch! Now, real swinging! When I was a boy . . ."

"Will you show me real swinging?" cried Littlenose.

"Wait here," said Uncle Redhead. Then he
walked back to the camp. He was back quickly,
carrying a large coil of raw-hide rope. Next he
scrabbled about in the undergrowth and dragged
out a piece of log. It was about the length of
Littlenose's arm, and as thick as his leg. Uncle
Redhead cut off two long lengths of rope before
walking amongst the trees and looking up at the
branches. Then he stopped, and slinging the
ropes over his shoulder, he began to climb. When
he reached a stout branch which grew out
sideways from the trunk high above the ground he
stopped and tied the ropes to it. Then he slid to
the ground and tied the other ends to the ends of
the log. The log swung gently to and fro at the
ends of the ropes.

"There's your swing," said Uncle Redhead. Littlenose just looked. "Sit on it," said Uncle Redhead. "Like this." And he sat on the log, held the ropes in his hands and pushed with his feet.

Littlenose stood open-mouthed as his uncle swung faster and faster, higher and higher. "Let *me* do it! Let *me* do it!" he cried.

Uncle Redhead got off. Littlenose got on . . . and promptly fell off again! But he soon got the hang of it, and Uncle Redhead pushed him as he swung higher and higher. Then he showed Littlenose how to make the swing go higher by himself by pulling on the ropes and pushing out with his legs. It was fantastic! Almost like flying. He soared up towards the tree-tops, and birds fluttered around his head in astonishment.

Back on the ground Uncle Redhead joined
Littlenose on the swing, standing with his feet
either side of Littlenose. Uncle Redhead made it
go higher than ever, and the two of them almost
shouted their heads off as they swooped and
rushed through the green leaves.

Father heard the shouting and wondered what was going on. He went to investigate, and almost fell over as Uncle Redhead and Littlenose suddenly swooshed down out of the tree-tops past Father's nose and swooshed up again. He looked for a moment, then with a: "More childish games! I might have known it!" he turned on his heel and went back to camp.

It was almost dark when Littlenose and Uncle Redhead returned to camp. They were having a bite of supper when Littlenose said, "I've been thinking. Why don't we wait until the pheasants have all gone to sleep then grab them!"

"A good question," said Uncle Redhead. "The trouble is that while pheasants run about on the ground, and feed on the ground, and even raise their young on the ground, they're not so stupid as to sleep on the ground. At nightfall they fly up into tall trees."

"Why can't we climb up after them?" said Littlenose.

"Because, even asleep, they can hear you as soon as you lay a finger on the tree. And spears are no good. It's difficult enough throwing a spear in the dark. It's impossible aiming it through the branches."

Littlenose fell asleep thinking about what
Uncle Redhead had said. And Father lay awake
thinking about what Uncle Redhead and
Littlenose had been doing. He wouldn't admit it
to anyone, but it had looked fun. He wouldn't
mind trying it himself. As long as no one were
looking, that is. He thought a bit more, then he
made up his mind. Littlenose and Uncle Redhead
were fast asleep. Father got quietly to his feet and
tiptoed away.

The moon shone brightly as Father picked his
way through the trees. Yes, there it was still, the
swing, swaying gently in the night breeze. With
some difficulty, Father balanced himself on the
log. He pushed off with his feet, gently at first,
then harder. He began to swing higher. He leaned
back and pushed as he had seen Littlenose and
Uncle Redhead do. And up and up he went. This
was exciting! The wind blew in his hair, and an
astonished owl gave a squeak of surprise as
Father swung up above the leaves. A family of
bats out hunting moths scattered in panic at the
strange apparition. A nightingale which had been
singing on a high bough broke off with a very
unmusical screech as Father suddenly appeared.

And it was at that moment that Father heard
the first ominous sound of a crack from the log!

Father was barely out of sight when Littlenose woke, he wasn't sure why. He sat up. Uncle Redhead was still snoring on the other side of the fire. But, where was Father? Littlenose looked again . . . then shook Uncle Redhead. "Father's gone," he shouted. "Maybe he's been eaten!" Without wasting a moment, Uncle Redhead grabbed his spear, jumped to his feet and headed for the trees.

Calling, "Father! Where are you?" Littlenose ran after his uncle. He followed him into the woods, and ran into him as he stopped. It was Father's voice. Coming from the sky: "HE-E-E-E-E-LP!"

As the log broke, Father lost his hold on the
ropes. They saw him do a neat double somersault
against the moon, then he was crashing his way
earthwards through the leaves, trying to grab a
hold to save himself.

With a resounding thump, Father landed in a
bush. In each hand he clutched a plump
pheasant, grabbed as he fell through the branches
where they roosted. Littlenose looked in
amazement. It was Father, not Uncle Redhead,
who had a special method for catching pheasants!
He said as much. But Father only grunted and
rubbed his sore back. It was a pity in a way that
Father had only managed one brace of pheasants,
thought Littlenose; but it was better than nothing
and Mother would make something quite
delicious with them.

With that happy thought he followed Father
and Uncle Redhead back to camp to finish his
interrupted sleep.

Journey to the End of the World

Littlenose was playing quietly outside the cave with Two-Eyes when he heard the tramp of feet and the sound of voices. It was a hunting party returning . . . and not a very successful one either.

In true Neanderthal fashion the hunters were shouting at each other, blaming everyone else for the lack of meat. At length, Nosey the chief tracker raised his voice. "Listen," he said, "there's no point in all this argument. We're empty-handed because you lot have no patience."

"What do you mean 'patience'?" said one of the hunters. "We trailed that woolly rhinoceros for three days without even getting a glimpse of it!"

"And we would have probably caught it on the fourth day if you hadn't given up!"

At this the hunters started shouting again, this time at Nosey. As they went off to their caves, Nosey shouted after them: "A proper hunter follows a trail to the end, even if that means to . . . to . . . to the end of the world!"

Littlenose heard all of this with great interest. He was due to go with a hunting party in a few days. One thing he was sure of: HE would follow any trail to the very end, no matter *where* it might be.

The day of the hunting party came. There were ten hunters in all, including Littlenose, eleven counting Two-Eyes. They left at dawn, Nosey leading with his remarkable nose. He walked along, head down, at the front of the column sniffing and snuffling. And by the end of the day it didn't seem likely that they would have a trail to follow as far as the next *tree*, let alone the end of the world. Nosey could not pick up a single scent! They camped for the night, and in the morning two of the hunters said that enough was enough and set off home.

The remaining eight went on after breakfast. Then their luck changed. Nosey suddenly held up his hand, and they all stopped while he dropped to his knees and examined the ground. He nodded wisely. "An elk," he said, "heading that way!" And he pointed. Much cheered, the hunters set off on the trail of the elk.

The elk had left a clear trail – at least to Nosey – and the hunters gripped their spears tightly in readiness. After a time they didn't grip them quite so tightly. Then they carried them under their arms, over their shoulders, in a very relaxed manner. Nosey raged at them. "Stay alert!" he shouted. "The elk may be just beyond that ridge."

But it wasn't. What *was* beyond the ridge was a river, flowing broad and swift. Two of the hunters sat down on the ground. A third threw a pebble into the water. "Well, that's it," he cried. "We can't follow a trail in running water. I'm off. Coming?" The other two stood up and followed him as he retraced their route back over the ridge in the direction of home.

Nosey said nothing. While everyone else sat on the ground and rested, he waded across the river, feeling his way with his spear. On the far bank he stooped and sniffed at the ground. He moved up and down the bank examining the grass and the riverside gravel. Then he gave a loud shout, and they saw him waving from a patch of sandy shore downstream on the opposite bank.

"I've found the trail!" he cried. "The elk must have waded downstream to throw us off the scent! It's an old trick . . . but no problem to an expert!"

What was left of the hunting party waded across. Sure enough, as Nosey had said, there were hoof prints in the soft sand. The elk had even left a clear trail in the long grass beyond the river, not needing Nosey's wonderful nose to follow it. The hunters began to get excited. They began to run. They had been running for some time before they realised that they were no longer on grass. The land was rising to a range of hills, and the ground had changed to flat rock with patches of gravel. The run slowed to a trot, then to a walk. Then they stood and looked at Nosey, who scratched his head.

It was now mid-afternoon. They would have to find a camping place soon, and as no one fancied sleeping on hard rock they agreed to go on. If they happened to catch up with the elk, well and good, but their main concern now was somewhere to sleep. The rocky ground gave way to a grassy valley. Again Nosey held up his hand to halt the party. "Have you found the trail?" they asked.

"Better than that," said Nosey quietly. "I've found the elk. The trail leads right into that patch of long grass and bushes. I saw a movement a moment ago." Cautiously, the hunters crept towards the patch of long grass and bushes. "Ready, men," whispered Nosey. "We'll surprise it!"

But it was the hunters who got the surprise!

With a crash of branches and a thunder of hooves, out burst an enormous and very angry woolly rhinoceros. It was having a quiet rest in the shade when this bunch of idiotic Neanderthal men had come creeping up, whispering among themselves and generally being a nuisance. The hunters scattered in all directions, and eventually the rhinoceros decided that they had been frightened enough and trotted away with a swish of its tail.

Even that wasn't the end of their troubles. They were just getting their breath back when Littlenose said, "I'm sure I felt rain."

He had scarcely spoken when there was a bright flash of lightning, a crash of thunder, and the rain cascaded from the clouds. The valley was bare of any kind of shelter, but Littlenose pointed to the hillside. There was a dark opening which might just be a cave. And it was. They scrambled panting into the shelter of the rocky opening. It was a tight squeeze, but at least they were out of the rain. There was some dead wood in the cave, and they lit a fire. And when they were more or less dry again they held a council of war.

"As I see it," said one man, "we're just wasting our time. We've followed this invisible elk for the better part of three days with nothing to show for it. I propose that we call it a day, and go home as soon as it's light in the morning."

"But we've come so far," cried Nosey. "We can't give up now!"

"Oh, yes we can," said another hunter. "Easy as falling off a log."

"Hands up all those who want to carry on," said Nosey, putting his own hand up.

Nobody moved . . . except Littlenose. He held up his hand. "I'll come with you, Mr Nosey," he said. "And Two-Eyes."

"I wish he'd mind his own business," thought Two-Eyes to himself. Nevertheless he raised his trunk.

"Right," said Nosey. "That's it. And won't you lot be sorry when we bring home the elk."

Next morning the party split up. The three hunters set off home, while Nosey, Littlenose and Two-Eyes made ready to take up the trail of the elk.

Nosey sniffed and snuffled his way up the valley, while Littlenose kept a wary eye open for the rhinoceros. Then Nosey gave a cry of delight. "I've found it! Here's the trail."

They pressed on. The trail led them up the valley and into another. The hills rose higher on either side. The clouds hadn't cleared after the storm and lay low on the tops of the hills. Now they were following the course of another river. It was very broad and flowed smoothly between rocky banks. Mist began to drift down from the hills. The air grew heavy. And even though the trail now led through thick woods that lined the river-bank, there was no bird-song.

Two-Eyes looked nervously about him as he hurried after Littlenose. And Littlenose kept as close as possible to Nosey. They stopped to rest for a moment. It was absolutely silent. Even the river made no sound as it slid, dark and smooth, between its banks. The trees were all leafless, and their feet moved noiselessly on the damp mossy ground. Then the mist began to close in. The sky was bright overhead, but at ground level there was only a sort of twilight.

But still the elk trail led on. Over the damp ground and through the silent woods. "These tracks are fresh," said Nosey. "We can't be far behind." And Littlenose could see clearly the cloven hoof marks in the ground. Then they came at last to the edge of the trees, and there it was!

The shape of the beast loomed out of the mist. The faint light caught the spread of its antlers. It wheeled round as it caught the Neanderthal scent, and took a step forward. Nosey was an expert hunter. His spear was at the ready. Taking a quick aim he threw it straight and fast.

"Well done, Mr Nosey," said Littlenose in a hushed voice. It seemed an odd thing to do. He should have shouted for joy at a successful hunt. But not in this strange place.

They loaded the dead elk onto Two-Eyes, and
were just about to go when Littlenose said,
"Look! Over here!"

Nosey joined him where he stood on a rocky
outcrop above the river. The river, without a
ripple, plunged over a mighty waterfall and
vanished into the mist. They couldn't see the
bottom. Littlenose threw a stone over the edge,
but they waited in vain for the sound of its fall.

Nosey and Littlenose looked at each other and shivered. What was this strange place of mist and silence and a great river which vanished into darkness without a sound?

Turning their backs on the falls, they made their way through the silent woods. Soon they were out in the open valley, and the day grew brighter as they left the mist behind. Birds began to sing. And even Two-Eyes gave a squeak as if he were glad to be away from the gloom and silence and on the way home.

They were passing the cave where they had found shelter from the storm when Littlenose paused. "Mr Nosey," he said, "I've been thinking. We did what you said. We followed the trail right to the end. I know what that place was! *That* was the *end of the world*."

Nosey was silent for a moment. Then he nodded slowly. "You know, Littlenose? I think you may be right."

And they started on the long march back to the caves and their own people.

Rock-a-Bye Littlenose

Night had fallen, and in the caves of the
Neanderthal Folk everyone was asleep. Except
Littlenose. He tossed and he turned. He sat up in
bed and lay down again. "For goodness' sake,
Littlenose," shouted Father, "go to sleep! You're
keeping everyone awake!"

This wasn't quite true, however, as Mother was
only awake because Father was shouting, and
Two-Eyes was fast asleep in a corner.

"I can't get to sleep," said Littlenose. "My
bed's full of bumps and wrinkles!"

"If you made your bed properly every morning
as Mother tells you," said Father, "this sort of
thing wouldn't happen!"

Littlenose lay down and pulled the covers over his head and, surprisingly, was soon fast asleep.

When Littlenose woke next morning he ached all over. "It's your own fault," said Mother. "You can spend this morning airing and shaking your bed and re-making it properly." A Neanderthal bed was a pile of bear skins and other furs which served as both mattress and covers and was spread on the floor of the cave.

Littlenose began to drag his bedding out into the middle of the cave. It was quite remarkable what came to light, and even more remarkable that he managed to sleep at all. There was an old flint knife and some lucky coloured pebbles in the folds of one fur. Lifting up another, an apple core and a couple of old bones tumbled out – the remains of a midnight snack. At the very bottom of the heap a particularly hard lump was revealed as a spare fire-making flint. It was exciting! Like a treasure hunt!

"Now," said Mother, "get those furs outside
and beat them until they are clean." And
Littlenose laid out the furs on a rock and beat
them vigorously with a long stick. He raised
clouds of dust. When Mother was satisfied that
the bedding was clean and fresh, Littlenose
wearily carried it back into the cave to his own
special corner.

Then he called to Two-Eyes and together they made their way to Littlenose's favourite tree where they did their more important thinking.

Littlenose said, "You know, Two-Eyes, people are pretty unreasonable. Sleeping on the floor, I mean. It's all right for you. With your fur you could sleep on a bed of thistles without even noticing." He leaned back and watched a bird

disappear into the foliage above his head. "Now, birds have more sense," he said. "No lying on the hard ground for them; they build nests with wool and feathers and things to line them. And I bet *they* never lose a single wink of sleep." Suddenly he leapt to his feet and shouted: "I'VE GOT IT, TWO-EYES!"

Startled, Two-Eyes jumped sideways and gave Littlenose a suspicious look. Littlenose's ideas usually spelt trouble for someone – more often than not for Two-Eyes. He sneaked away as Littlenose paced up and down waving his arms as he explained his great idea.

"People nests!" he said. "If people had nests like the birds, there would be none of this business of hard floors. At bed-time they would simply snuggle down and be lulled to sleep by the gentle swaying of the branches." There and then he decided to build a "people nest", or, rather, a "boy nest" to prove that it could be done.

From the sun, Littlenose judged that it was almost lunch-time, but there was a lot he could do before then. He had to find a suitable tree, for instance. He set off into the woods.

He was deep in the forest before he found what he was looking for. A tall straight tree with plenty of hand- and foot-holds for climbing, and right at the top a stout limb growing straight out from the trunk with a large fork at the end. He started to gather twigs and branches for his nest. The time flew past, and Littlenose forgot completely that he should have been home for lunch.

Then came the tricky part, getting the twigs and branches to the top of the tree and building the nest. Littlenose could only carry one branch at a time as he climbed carefully to the fork. Soon his limbs ached and he was scratched and sore. The branches seemed to get heavier and heavier, but in the end the last one was up and carefully balanced with the others across the forked branch.

Then he took his flint knife out of his furs and carefully cut strips of bark about as long as his forearm and as broad as his finger. He began to arrange the nesting material across the fork, using the strips of bark to lash it firmly in place. Slowly the nest began to take shape. It was bowl-shaped and beginning to look very nest-like when he realised that he had run out of twigs. He didn't need many. Just enough leafy ones to make a soft and comfortable lining. He slid back along the branch to the trunk and broke off all the leafy branches he could reach and threw them into the nest. Then he hung down and collected more from lower down. It was a simple matter to arrange them inside the woven branches – and the job was done. Littlenose looked at his handiwork with pride. Carefully he lay down on the soft leaves. He watched the clouds drift across the sky. The nest rocked gently in the tree-top. And Littlenose fell asleep!

When Littlenose didn't turn up at lunch-time Mother was angry. But when there was still no sign of him at supper-time she became worried. For Littlenose to miss two meals in a row was most unusual. Then Father came home, and a full-scale search was mounted. With some reluctance and a lot of muttering, the search party assembled in the gathering dusk.

"If that boy were mine," grumbled one man, "I'd throw him to the bears!"

"They'd throw him right back," said another. "Bears have more sense!"

They were just leaving when a strange figure
stumbled into the circle of torch-light. It was an
old, old man. He carried a bundle of sticks in one
shaking hand as he lurched and stumbled into the
midst of the search party. He grabbed one man by
the arm and wheezed and puffed, trying to speak
and get his wind back at the same time.

"It's old Nod," said Father. "What on earth's
the matter with him?" Nod was a simple old
man who spent most of his time collecting herbs.
He had evidently been gathering firewood
in the forest.

After a moment Nod calmed down a bit and stopped gasping. Then he pointed dramatically back the way he had come and cried, "Big as a mammoth! Out of the sky! It'll have us all!"

"What will?" asked Father.

"IT!" cried Nod. And he darted about flapping his arms like wings and talking so fast that only one word in ten made sense. Then they realised what Nod was telling them. He'd fled for his life from a giant bird! No, he hadn't actually *seen* a giant bird; but he had seen a giant *nest*! What more did they want?

"Could you lead us to it?" asked Father. Nod was perhaps simple, but he was not stupid. Bringing word of a ferocious giant bird in the forest was one thing – going back for another look was something else altogether. He gathered up his firewood and hurried off towards his cave.

"Silly old man," said Father. "Probably imagined the whole thing! Come on. We've wasted enough time as it is." And off they set on their delayed hunt for the missing Littlenose. By the light of their torches, the search party peered into the shadows and prodded the undergrowth with their spears, but of Littlenose there was no sign. "You don't suppose the giant bird got him?" said someone.

"You don't believe that nonsense, do you?" said Father, and he started to laugh. But no one else did!

The moon had risen, and Father realised that the others were not even looking at him. They were gazing across a clearing to where a tall tree grew slightly separate from the rest. Their eyes travelled up the trunk. Up and up to where a large branch grew out near the top. And there they saw it. There could be no doubt. It was a nest. But, what a nest!

"What do we do now?" they asked each other.

Littlenose woke with a start. He hadn't meant to
sleep, and now it was dark. He climbed out of his
nest and slid along the branch to the trunk of the
tree. He felt in the light of the moon for foot- and
hand-holds. And there were none! Where were all
the branches he had used to climb up? Then he
remembered. The leafy branches he had broken
off to make a comfortable lining were the very
branches he had used. He was stuck. He got back
into the nest, took a deep breath, and shouted:
"HELP!"

To his amazement there was an immediate
reply. A voice out of the darkness shouted, "HI!"
Then other voices joined in, including Father's.
They were all talking at once. Mainly nonsense,
by the sound. "It's Littlenose! It must have got
him! Do you think he's all right? Are you all right,
Littlenose?"

"Yes," cried Littlenose. "But I can't get down."

"Hang on!" shouted Father and, slinging a coil of raw-hide rope around his shoulders, he began to climb the tree. He reached the last of the hand-holds, balanced himself as best he could, and tied one end of the rope around his waist. "Tie the end to the branch," he called, throwing the coiled rope to Littlenose. Littlenose did so, and waited to see what Father intended to do next. He never knew, because at that moment Father lost his balance and with a horrible yell vanished into the darkness. The search party scattered as Father plummeted towards them. But the rope had got into a great tangle and Father was brought up short half-way to the ground, dangling helplessly. "Don't all just stand there," he cried. "Get me down!"

"I'll get you down," came Littlenose's voice.

Father looked up. "No, not THAT!" he cried.

Littlenose was clinging to the branch and
sawing at the raw-hide rope with his flint knife.
"Almost there," he called encouragingly. And
before Father could utter another protest the rope
parted. For the second time Father hurtled
groundwards. He collided head-on with one of the
search party. Luckily, Neanderthal heads were
made for rough treatment. Even as they tumbled
in a heap, another body crashed amongst them.
Suddenly relieved of Father's weight, the branch
had sprung upwards, catapulting Littlenose into
the air. The piled-up search party broke his fall
safely, if a bit abruptly.

They got to their feet, picked up the scattered
torches and looked at Littlenose. "Look at those
scratches," they said. "Must be claw marks. Or
beak marks. What an experience!"

Father said, "We'd better not hang around in case it comes back." And off they hurried with Littlenose, not even scolding him for all the bother he'd caused. It was all very strange. Mother even burst into tears when he got home.

Still bewildered, Littlenose found himself washed, fed and tucked up in bed. And of one thing he was now certain. Nests were so much trouble that anyone who preferred a nest to a good solid floor must be positively bird-brained!

Well done, Littlenose!

And so, Littlenose became a Junior Hunter.
Naturally, Father and Mother were extremely
proud of him. And Littlenose himself went
around feeling twice as tall for several days after.
But, when he thought about it (sitting under his
favourite tree, of course), he knew that he would
never have done it without the help of Father and
Nosey and all the others who had taught him
everything he knew about hunting. And he had to
admit that without Two-Eyes he might never have
passed his final test at all.

It was an important lesson for Littlenose. In
dangerous times like the Ice Age people couldn't
survive without the help of others.

Perhaps it's different today. Or is it? What do
you think?

100,000 YEARS AGO people wore no clothes. They lived in caves and hunted animals for food. They were called NEANDERTHAL.

50,000 YEARS AGO when Littlenose lived, clothes were made out of fur. But now there were other people. Littlenose called them Straightnoses. Their proper name is HOMO SAPIENS.

5,000 YEARS AGO there were no Neanderthal people left. People wore cloth as well as fur. They built in wood and stone. They grew crops and kept cattle.

1,000 YEARS AGO towns were built, and men began to travel far from home by land and sea to explore the world.

500 YEARS AGO towns became larger, as did the ships in which men travelled. The houses they built were very like those we see today.

100 YEARS AGO people used machines to do a lot of the harder work. They could now travel by steam train. Towns and cities became very big, with factories as well as houses.

TODAY we don't hunt for our food, but buy it in shops. We travel by car and aeroplane. Littlenose would not understand any of this. Would YOU like to live as Littlenose did?

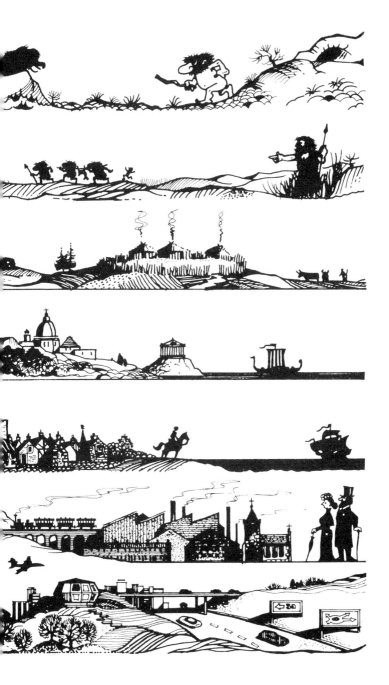

95

Other Books about Littlenose